Dumpling and Other Stories

Dick King-Smith

Illustrated by
Michael Terry

PUFFIN BOOKS

PUFFIN BOOKS

Published by the Penguin Group
Penguin Books Ltd, 27 Wrights Lane, London W8 5TZ, England
Penguin Books USA Inc., 375 Hudson Street, New York, New York 10014, USA
Penguin Books Australia Ltd, Ringwood, Victoria, Australia
Penguin Books Canada Ltd, 10 Alcorn Avenue, Toronto, Ontario, Canada M4V 3B2
Penguin Books (NZ) Ltd, 182–190 Wairau Road, Auckland 10, New Zealand

Penguin Books Ltd, Registered Offices: Harmondsworth, Middlesex, England

Dumpling first published by Hamish Hamilton Ltd 1990
Published as *Blessu and Dumpling* in Puffin Books 1992
Text copyright © Fox Busters Ltd, 1992

'Keep yelling, young un' from *The Sheep-Pig*
first published by Victor Gollancz Ltd 1983
Published in Puffin Books 1985
Text copyright © Dick King-Smith, 1983

'The Excitement of Being Ernest' from A *Narrow Squeak and Other Animal Stories*
first published by Viking 1993
Published in Puffin Books 1995
Text copyright © Fox Busters Ltd, 1993

This edition published in Puffin Books 1997
1 3 5 7 9 10 8 6 4 2

Illustrations copyright © Michael Terry, 1997
Filmset in Monotype Baskerville

Manufactured in China by Imago Ltd
British Library Cataloguing in Publication Data
A CIP catalogue record for this book is available from the British Library

ISBN 0-140-38718-8

Contents

Dumpling

'OH, HOW I long to be long!' said Dumpling.

'Who do you want to belong to?' asked one of her brothers.

'No, I don't mean *to belong,*' said Dumpling. 'I mean, to BE LONG!'

When the three dachshund puppies had been born, they had looked much like pups of any other breed.

Then, as they became older, the two brothers began to grow long, as dachshunds do. Their noses moved further and further away from their tail-tips.

But the third puppy stayed short and stumpy.

1

'How *long* you are getting,' said the lady who owned them all to the two brothers.

She called one of them Joker because he was always playing silly games, and the other one Thinker, because he liked to sit and think deeply.

Then she looked at their sister and shook her head.

'You are nice and healthy,' she said. 'Your eyes are bright and your coat is shining and you're good and plump. But dachshunds are supposed to have long bodies, you know. And you haven't. You're just a little dumpling.'

Dumpling asked her mother about the problem.

'Will I ever grow really long like Joker and Thinker?' she asked.

Her mother looked at her plump daughter and sighed.

'Time will tell,' she said.

Dumpling asked her brother, Joker.

'Joker,' she said. 'How can I grow longer?'

'That's easy, Dumpy,' said Joker. 'I'll hold

your nose and Thinker will hold your tail
and we'll stretch you.'

'Don't be silly, Joker,' said Thinker.

Thinker was a serious puppy. He did not
like to play jokes. 'It would hurt Dumpy if
we did that.'

'Well then, what shall I do, Thinker?'
asked Dumpling.

Thinker thought deeply. Then he said,
'Try going for long walks. And it helps if you
take very long steps.'

So Dumpling set off the next morning. All

the dachshunds were out in the garden. The puppies' mother was snoozing in the sunshine.

Joker was playing a silly game pretending that a stick was a snake.

Thinker was sitting and thinking deeply.

Dumpling slipped away through a hole in the hedge.

Next to the garden was a wood, and she set off between the trees on her very short legs. She stepped out boldly, trying hard to imagine herself growing a tiny bit longer with each step.

Suddenly she bumped into a large black cat which was sitting under a yew tree.

'Oh, I beg your pardon!' said Dumpling.

'Granted,' said the cat. 'Where are you going?'

'Oh, nowhere special. I'm just taking a long walk. You see, I'm trying to grow longer,' and she went on to explain about dachshunds and how they should look.

'Everyone calls me Dumpling,' she said sadly. 'I wish I could be long.'

'Granted,' said the black cat again.

'What do you mean?' she said. 'Can you make me long?'

'Easy as winking,' said the cat, winking. 'I'm a witch's cat. I'll cast a spell on you. How long do you want to be?'

'Oh, very, very long!' cried Dumpling excitedly. 'The longest dachshund ever!'

The black cat stared at her with his green eyes, and then he shut them and began to chant:

'Abra-cat-abra,
Hark to my song,
It will make you
Very long.'

The sound of the cat's voice died away and the wood was suddenly very still.

Then the cat gave himself a shake and opened his eyes.

'Remember,' he said, 'you asked for it.'

'Oh, thank you, thank you!' said Dumpling. 'I feel longer already. Will I see you again?'

'I shouldn't wonder,' said the cat.

Dumpling set off back towards the garden. The feeling of growing longer was lovely. She wagged her tail madly, and each wag seemed a little further away than the last.

She thought how surprised Joker and Thinker would be. She would be much longer than they.

'Dumpling, indeed!' she said. 'I will have to have a new name now, a very long one to match my new body.'

But then she began to find walking difficult. Her front feet knew where they were going, but her back feet acted very oddly. They seemed to be a long way behind her.

They kept tripping over things, and dropping into rabbit-holes.

They kept getting stuck among the bushes. She couldn't see her tail, so she went round a big tree to look for it and met it on the other side.

By now, she was wriggling on her tummy like a snake.

'Help!' yapped Dumpling at the top of her voice. 'Cat, come back, please!'

'Granted,' said the witch's cat, appearing suddenly beside her. 'What's the trouble now?'

'Oh, please,' cried Dumpling, 'undo your spell!'

'Some people are never satisfied,' said the cat. Once more he stared at her with his green eyes.

Then he shut them and began to chant:

'Abra-cat-abra,
Hear my song,
It will make you
Short not long.'

Dumpling never forgot how wonderful it felt as her back feet came towards her front ones, and her tummy rose from the ground.

She hurried homewards, and squeezed her nice, comfortable, short, stumpy body through the hole in the hedge.

Joker and Thinker came galloping across the grass towards her.

How clumsy they look, she thought, with those silly long bodies.

'Where have you been, Dumpy?' shouted Joker.

'Did the exercise make you longer?' asked Thinker.

'No,' said Dumpling. 'But as a matter of fact, I'm quite happy as I am now.

'And that's about the long and the short of it!'

'Keep yelling, young un'

MRS HOGGET SHOOK her head at least a dozen times.

'For the life of me I can't see why you do let that pig run all over the place like you do, round and round the yard he do go, chasing my ducks about, shoving his nose into everything, shouldn't wonder but what he'll be out with you and Fly moving the sheep about afore long, why dussen't shut him up, he's running all his flesh off, he won't never be fit for Christmas, Easter more like, what d'you call him?'

'Just Pig,' said Farmer Hogget.

A month had gone by since the Village

Fair, a month in which a lot of interesting things had happened to Babe. The fact that perhaps most concerned his future, though he did not know it, was that Farmer Hogget had become fond of him. He liked to see the piglet pottering happily about the yard with Fly, keeping out of mischief, as far as he could tell, if you didn't count moving the ducks around. He did this now with a good deal of skill, the farmer noticed, even to the extent of being able, once, to separate the white ducks from the brown, though that must just have been a fluke. The more he thought of it, the less Farmer Hogget liked the idea of butchering Pig.

The other developments were in Babe's education. Despite herself, Fly found that she took pleasure and pride in teaching him the ways of the sheep-dog, though she knew that of course he would never be fast enough to work sheep. Anyway the boss would never let him try.

As for Ma, she was back with the flock, her foot healed, her cough better. But all the

12

time that she had been shut in the box,
Babe had spent every moment that Fly was
out of the stables chatting to the old ewe.
Already he understood, in a way that Fly
never could, the sheep's point of view. He
longed to meet the flock, to be introduced.
He thought it would be extremely
interesting.

'D'you think I could, Ma?' he had said.

'Could what, young un?'

'Well, come and visit you, when you go back to your friends?'

'Oh ar. You could do, easy enough. You only got to go through the bottom gate and up the hill to the big field by the lane. Don't know what the farmer'd say though. Or that wolf.'

Once Fly had slipped quietly in and found him perched on the straw stack.

'Babe!' she had said sharply. 'You're not talking to that stupid thing, are you?'

'Well, yes, Mum, I was.'

'Save your breath, dear. It won't understand a word you say.'

'Bah!' said Ma.

For a moment Babe was tempted to tell his foster-mother what he had in mind, but something told him to keep quiet. Instead he made a plan. He would wait for two things to happen. First, for Ma to rejoin the flock. And after that for market day, when both the boss and his mum would be out of the way. Then he would go up the hill.

Towards the end of the very next week the two things had happened. Ma had been turned out, and a couple of days after that Babe watched as Fly jumped into the back of the Land Rover, and it drove out of the yard and away.

Babe's were not the only eyes that watched its departure. At the top of the hill a cattle-lorry stood half-hidden under a clump of trees at the side of the lane. As soon as the Land-Rover had disappeared from sight along the road to the market town, a man jumped hurriedly out and opened the gate into the field. Another backed the lorry into the gateway.

Babe meanwhile was trotting excitedly up the hill to pay his visit to the flock. He came to the gate at the bottom of the field and squeezed under it. The field was steep and curved, and at first he could not see a single sheep. But then he heard a distant drumming of hooves and suddenly the whole flock came galloping over the brow of the hill and down towards him. Around them ran two strange collies, lean silent dogs that seemed to flow effortlessly over the grass. From high above came the sound of a thin whistle, and in easy partnership the dogs swept round the sheep, and began to drive them back up the slope.

Despite himself, Babe was caught up in the press of jostling bleating animals and carried along with them. Around him rose a

chorus of panting protesting voices, some
shrill, some hoarse, some deep and guttural,
but all saying the same thing.

'Wolf! Wolf!' cried the flock in dazed
confusion.

Small by comparison and short in the leg,
Babe soon fell behind the main body, and as
they reached the top of the hill he found
himself right at the back in company with

an old sheep who cried 'Wolf!' more loudly than any.

'Ma!' he cried breathlessly. 'It's you!'

Behind them one dog lay down at a whistle, and in front the flock checked as the other dog steadied them. In the corner of the field the tailboard and wings of the cattle-lorry filled the gateway, and the two men waited, sticks and arms outspread.

'Oh, hullo, young un,' puffed the old sheep. 'Fine day you chose to come, I'll say.'

'What is it? What's happening? Who are these men?' asked Babe.

'Rustlers,' said Ma. 'They'm sheep-rustlers.'

'What d'you mean?'

'Thieves, young un, that's what I do mean. Sheep-stealers. We'll all be in thik lorry afore you can blink your eye.'

'What can we do?'

'Do? Ain't nothing we can do, unless we can slip past theseyer wolf.'

She made as if to escape, but the dog behind darted in, and she turned back.

Again, one of the men whistled, and the dog pressed. Gradually, held against the headland of the field by the second dog and the men, the flock began to move forward. Already the leaders were nearing the tailboard of the lorry.

'We'm beat,' said Ma mournfully. 'You run for it, young un.' I will, thought Babe, but not the way you mean. Little as he was, he felt suddenly not fear but anger, furious

anger that the boss's sheep were being
stolen. My mum's not here to protect them
so I must, he said to himself bravely, and he
ran quickly round the hedge side of the
flock, and jumping on to the bottom of the
tailboard, turned to face them.

'Please!' he cried. 'I beg you! Please don't
come any further. If you would be so kind,
dear sensible sheep!'

His unexpected appearance had a

number of immediate effects. The shock of being so politely addressed stopped the flock in its tracks, and the cries of 'Wolf!' changed to murmurs of 'In't he lovely!' and 'Proper little gennulman!' Ma had told them something of her new friend, and now to see him in the flesh and to hear his well-chosen words released them from the dominance of the dogs. They began to fidget and look about for an escape route. This was opened for them when the men (cursing quietly, for above all things they were anxious to avoid too much noise) sent the flanking dog to drive the pig away, and some of the sheep began to slip past them.

Next moment all was chaos. Angrily the dog ran at Babe, who scuttled away squealing at the top of his voice in a mixture of fright and fury. The men closed on him, sticks raised. Desperately he shot between the legs of one, who fell with a crash, while the other, striking out madly, hit the rearguard dog as it came to help, and sent it yowling. In half a minute the carefully planned raid was ruined, as the sheep scattered everywhere.

'Keep yelling, young un!' bawled Ma, as she ran beside Babe. 'They won't never stop here with that row going on!'

And suddenly all sorts of things began to happen as those deafening squeals rang out over the quiet countryside. Birds flew startled from the trees, cows in nearby fields began to gallop about, dogs in distant farms to bark, passing motorists to stop and stare. In the farmhouse below Mrs Hogget heard the noise as she had on the day of the Fair, but now it was infinitely louder, the most piercing, nerve-tingling, ear-shattering burglar alarm. She dialled 999 but then talked for so long that by the time a patrol car drove up the lane, the rustlers had long gone. Snarling at each other and their dogs, they had driven hurriedly away with not one single sheep to show for their pains.

'You won't never believe it!' cried Mrs Hogget when her husband returned from

market. 'But we've had rustlers, just after you'd gone it were, come with a girt cattle-lorry they did, the police said, they seen the tyremarks in the gateway, and a chap in a car seen the lorry go by in a hurry, and there's been a lot of it about, and he give the alarm, he did, kept screaming and shrieking enough to bust your eardrums, we should have lost every sheep on the place if 'tweren't for him, 'tis him we've got to thank.'

'Who?' said Farmer Hogget.

'Him!' said his wife, pointing at Babe who was telling Fly all about it. 'Don't ask me how he got there or why he done it, all I knows is he saved our bacon and now I'm going to save his, he's stopping with us just like another dog, don't care if he gets so big as a house, because if you think I'm going to stand by and see him butchered after what he done for us today, you've got another think coming, what d'you say to that?'

A slow smile spread over Farmer Hogget's long face.

The Excitement of Being Ernest

THE FIRST THING that struck you about
Ernest was his colour. If you had to put a
name to it, you would say 'honey' – not that
pale wax honey that needs a knife to get it
out of a jar, but the darker, richer, runny
stuff that drips all over the tablecloth if you
don't wind the spoon round it properly.

That was the colour of Ernest's coat, and
the second thing about him that was
remarkable was the amount of coat he
carried. He was very hairy. Body, legs, tail,
all had their fair share of that runny-honey-
coloured hair, but it was Ernest's face that
was his fortune, with its fine beard and

moustaches framed by shortish, droopy ears. From under bushy eyebrows, Ernest looked out upon the world and found it good. Only one thing bothered him. He did not know what kind of dog he was.

It should have been simple, of course, to find out. There were a number of other dogs living in the village who could presumably have told him, but somehow Ernest had never plucked up the courage to ask. To begin with, the other dogs all looked

so posh. They were all of different breeds, but each one appeared so obviously well bred, so self-assured, so upper class, that Ernest had always hesitated to approach them, least of all with a daft question like, 'Excuse me. I wonder if you could tell me what sort of dog I am?'

For that matter, he thought to himself one day, I don't even know what sort of dogs they are, and then it occurred to him that that would be a much more sensible question to ask and could lead perhaps to the kind of conversation about breeds in general where one of them might say, 'I'm a Thingummytite, and you, I see, are a Wotchermecallum.'

So after he had helped to get the cows in for morning milking on the farm where he lived, Ernest trotted up to the village to the gateway of the Manor House – an imposing entrance flanked by fine pillars – and peered in under his bushy eyebrows. Standing in the drive was the Manor House dog. Ernest lifted his leg politely on one of the fine stone pillars, and called out, 'Excuse me! I wonder if you could tell me what sort of dog you are?'

'Ich bin ein German Short-haired Pointer,' said the Manor House dog, 'if dot is any business of yours.'

'Oh,' said Ernest. 'I'm not one of those.'

He waited expectantly to be told what he was.

'Dot,' said the German Short-haired Pointer pointedly, 'is as plain as der nose on your face,' and he turned his back and walked away.

Ernest went on to the Vicarage, and saw, through the wicket-gate, the Vicar's dog lying on the lawn.

'Excuse me,' said Ernest, lifting his leg politely on the wicket-gate. 'I wonder if you could tell me what sort of dog you are?'

'Nom d'un chien!' said the Vicar's dog. 'Je suis un French Bulldog.'

'Oh,' said Ernest. 'I'm not one of those.'

The French Bulldog snorted, and though Ernest waited hopefully for a while, it said

nothing more, so he walked down the road
till he came to the pub.

The publican's dog was very large indeed,
and Ernest thought it best to keep some
distance away. He lifted his leg discreetly on
an empty beer barrel and shouted across the
pub car-park, 'Excuse me! I wonder if you
could tell me what sort of dog you are?'

'Oi'm an Irish Wolfhound,' said the
publican's dog in a deep, rumbly voice.

'Oh,' said Ernest. 'I'm not one of those.'

'Bedad you're not,' said the Irish

Wolfhound. 'Shall Oi be after tellin' yez what sort of a dog ye are?'

'Oh, yes please,' said Ernest eagerly.

'Sure ye're a misbegotten hairy mess,' said the Irish Wolfhound, 'and it's stinking of cow-muck ye are. Now bate it, if ye know what's good for you.'

Ernest beat it. But he wasn't beaten.

He paid a call on a number of houses in the village street, repeating his polite inquiry and receiving answers of varying degrees of rudeness from a Tibetan Terrier, an American Cocker Spaniel, a Finnish Spitz and a Chinese Crested Dog. But none of them volunteered any information as to what kind of animal he himself was.

There was one house left, by the junction of the road with the lane that led back to the farm, and standing outside it was a dog that Ernest had never seen before in the neighbourhood. It looked friendly and wagged its long, plumy tail as Ernest left his customary calling-card on the gate.

'Hello,' he said. 'I haven't seen you before.'

'We've only just moved in,' said the friendly stranger. 'You're the first dog I've met here, actually. Are there a lot in the village?'

'Yes.'

'Decent bunch?'

Ernest considered how best to answer this.

'They're all very well bred,' he said. 'I

imagine they've got pedigrees as long as your tail,' he added, 'like you have, I suppose?'

'You could say that,' replied the other. 'For what it's worth.'

Ernest sighed. I'll give it one more go, he thought.

'Straight question,' he said. 'What sort of dog are you?'

'Straight answer, English Setter.'

'English?' said Ernest delightedly. 'Well, that makes a change.'

'How do you mean?'

'Why, the rest of them are Chinese, German, Tibetan, Irish, American, Finnish – there's no end to the list.'

'Really? No, no I'm as English as you are.'

'Ah,' said Ernest carefully. 'Then you know what sort of dog I am?'

'Of course,' said the English Setter. 'You're a Gloucestershire Cow-dog.'

The hair over Ernest's face prevented the Setter from seeing the changing expression

that flitted across it, first of astonishment, then of excitement, and finally a studied look of smug satisfaction.

'Ah,' said Ernest. 'You knew. Not many do.'

'My dear chap,' said the Setter. 'You amaze me. I should have thought any dog would have recognized a Gloucestershire Cow-dog immediately.'

'Really?' said Ernest. 'Well, I suppose any English dog would.'

'Yes, that must be it. Anyway you'll be able to compete with all these pedigree chaps next week.'

'Why, what's happening next week?'

'It's the Village Fête.'

'Oh, I don't go to that sort of thing,' said Ernest. 'I've got too much work to do with the cows.'

'Quite. But this year there's a new attraction, apparently. They've just put the posters up, haven't you seen?'

'Didn't notice,' said Ernest.

'Well, there's one stuck on our wall. Come and have a look.'

And this is what they saw.

VILLAGE FÊTE
Saturday June 15th
By kind permission, in the grounds
of the Manor House

Skittle Alley
Coconut Shy
Cake Stall
Jam and Preserve Stall
White Elephant Stall
Hoopla
Wellie-throwing Competition
Guess the Weight of the Pig
Grand Dog Show

'But that's no good,' said Ernest. 'With all the pedigree dogs in the village, the judge will never look twice at me.'

*

'But that's no good,' said Sally. 'With all the pedigree dogs in the village, the judge will never look twice at Ernest.' Sally was the farmer's daughter, and she was looking at another of the notices, tacked on the farm gate.

'Oh, I don't know,' said her father. 'You might be surprised. Have a go. It's only a bit of fun. You'll have to clean him up a bit, mind.'

So when the great day dawned, Ernest ran to Sally's whistle after morning milking and found himself, to his surprise and disgust, required to stand in an old tin bath and be soaked and lathered and scrubbed and hosed, and then blow-dried with Sally's mother's electric drier plugged into a power point in the dairy.

'He looks a treat,' said the farmer and his wife when Sally had finished combing out that long, honey-coloured coat. And he did.

Indeed when they all arrived at the Fête, a number of people had difficulty in recognizing Ernest without his usual

covering of cow-muck. But the dogs weren't
fooled. Ernest heard them talking among
themselves as the competitors began to
gather for the Dog Show, and their
comments made his head drop and his tail
droop.

'Well I'll be goshdarned!' said the
American Cocker Spaniel to the Tibetan
Terrier. 'Will ya look at that mutt! Kinda
tough to have to share a show-ring with no-
account trash like that.'

And, turning to the Finnish Spitz, 'Velly

distlessing,' said the Chinese Crested Dog. 'No pediglee.'

'Ma foi!' said the French Bulldog to the Irish Wolfhound. 'Regardez zis 'airy creature! 'E is, 'ow you say, mongrel?'

'Begorrah, it's the truth ye're spakin,' said the Irish Wolfhound in his deep, rumbly voice, 'and it's stinking of soap powder he is.'

As for the German Short-haired Pointer, he made sure, seeing that he was host for the day, that his comment on Ernest's arrival on the croquet lawn (which was the show-ring) was heard by all.

'Velcome to der Manor, ladies and gentlemen,' he said to the other dogs. 'May der best-bred dog vin,' and he turned his back on Ernest in a very pointed way.

'Don't let them get you down, old chap,' said a voice in Ernest's ear, and there, standing next to him, was the friendly English Setter, long, plumy tail wagging.

'Oh, hello,' said Ernest in a doleful voice. 'Nice to see you. I hope you win, anyway. I haven't got a chance.'

'Oh, I don't know,' said the English Setter. 'You might be surprised. Have a go. It's only a bit of fun.'

He lowered his voice. 'Take a tip though, old chap. Don't lift your leg. It's not done.'

Suddenly Ernest felt much happier. He gave himself a good shake, and then, when they all began to parade around the ring, he stepped out smartly at Sally's side, his long (clean) honey-coloured coat shining in the summer sunshine.

The judge examined each entry in turn, looking in their mouths, feeling their legs and their backs, studying them from all angles, and making them walk up and down, just as though it was a class in a Championship Show.

When her turn came, he said to Sally, 'What's your dog called?'

'Ernest.'

From under bushy eyebrows, Ernest looked out upon the judge.

'Hello, Ernest,' the judge said, and then hesitated, because there was one thing that bothered him. He did not know what kind of dog Ernest was.

'You don't see many of these,' he said to Sally.

'Oh yes you do. There are lots about.'

'Lots of . . .?'

'Gloucestershire Cow-dogs.'

'Of course, of course,' said the judge.

When he had carefully examined all the entries, he made them walk round once more, and then he called out the lady of the Manor with her German Short-haired Pointer. When they came eagerly forward,

trying not to look too smug, he said, 'I've finished with you, thank you.'

And he called out, one after another, the Chinese Crested Dog and the Tibetan Terrier and the American Cocker Spaniel and the French Bulldog and the Irish Wolfhound and, to finish with, the Finnish Spitz, and said to each in turn, 'I've finished with you, thank you.'

Until the only dogs left on the croquet lawn were the English Setter and Ernest.

And the judge looked thoughtfully at both of them for quite a time before he straightened up and spoke to the owner of the English Setter.

'A very close thing,' he said, 'but I'm giving the first prize to the Gloucestershire Cow-dog,' and he walked across to the Vicar whose job it was to make all the announcements on the public address system.

'Well done, old boy,' said the English Setter. 'It couldn't have happened to a nicer chap.'

'But I don't understand,' said Ernest. 'How could I have won? Against all you aristocratic fellows that are registered with the Kennel Club, and have lots of champions in your pedigrees?'

'Listen,' said the English Setter as the Tannoy began to crackle and the voice of the Vicar boomed across the gardens of the Manor House.

'Ladies and gentlemen! We have the result of our Grand Dog Show! It's not quite

like Crufts, ha, ha – we do things a bit
differently down here – and in our Show
there has been only one class, for The Most
Lovable Dog. And the winner is . . . Ernest,
the Gloucestershire Cow-dog!'

And Sally gave Ernest a big hug, and the
judge gave Sally a little cup, and the English
Setter wagged his plumy tail like mad, and
everybody clapped like billy-o, and Ernest
barked and barked so loudly that he must
have been heard by nearly every cow in
Gloucestershire.

Oh, the excitement of being Ernest!